Dear Parent:
Your child's love of reading starts here!

P9-DCN-189

Every child learns to read in a different way and at his or her own speed. Some go back and forth between reading levels and read favorite books again and again. Others read through each level in order. You can help your young reader improve and become more confident by encouraging his or her own interests and abilities. From books your child reads with you to the first books he or she reads alone, there are I Can Read Books for every stage of reading:

SHARED READING
Basic language, word repetition, and whimsical illustrations, ideal for sharing with your emergent reader

BEGINNING READING
Short sentences, familiar words, and simple concepts for children eager to read on their own

READING WITH HELP
Engaging stories, longer sentences, and language play for developing readers

READING ALONE
Complex plots, challenging vocabulary, and high-interest topics for the independent reader

ADVANCED READING
Short paragraphs, chapters, and exciting themes for the perfect bridge to chapter books

I Can Read Books have introduced children to the joy of reading since 1957. Featuring award-winning authors and illustrators and a fabulous cast of beloved characters, I Can Read Books set the standard for beginning readers.

A lifetime of discovery begins with the magical words **"I Can Read!"**

Visit www.icanread.com for information
on enriching your child's reading experience.

I Can Read Book® is a trademark of HarperCollins Publishers.

Batman versus Man-Bat
Copyright © 2012 DC Comics.
BATMAN and all related characters and elements are trademarks of and © DC Comics.
(s12)

HARP2570
All rights reserved. Manufactured in China. No part of this book may be used or reproduced in any manner whatsoever without written permission except in the case of brief quotations embodied in critical articles and reviews. For information address HarperCollins Children's Books, a division of HarperCollins Publishers, 195 Broadway, New York, NY 10007.
www.harpercollinschildrens.com

Library of Congress catalog card number: 2011945753
ISBN 978-0-06-188523-5

Book design by John Sazaklis

14 15 16 17 18   SCP   10 9 8   ❖   First Edition

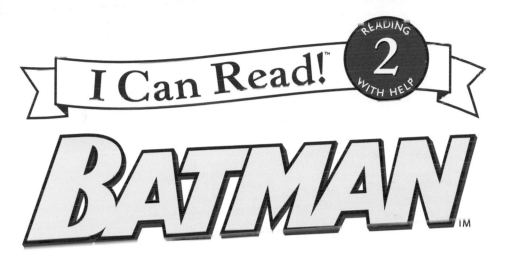

Batman versus Man-Bat

by J. E. Bright

pictures by Steven E. Gordon

colors by Eric A. Gordon

BATMAN created by Bob Kane

HARPER
An Imprint of HarperCollinsPublishers

BATMAN

Batman fights crime in Gotham City. He wears a mask and a cape. He is the World's Greatest Detective.

COMMISSIONER GORDON

James W. Gordon is the commissioner of the Gotham City Police Department. He is a dedicated police detective and trusted friend of Batman.

MAN-BAT

Before turning into Man-Bat, Dr. Kirk Langstrom was a scientist and an expert on bats. Desperate to stop his growing hearing loss, Langstrom created a special serum that he tested on himself. Instead of curing him, the chemical turned him into a man-sized bat.

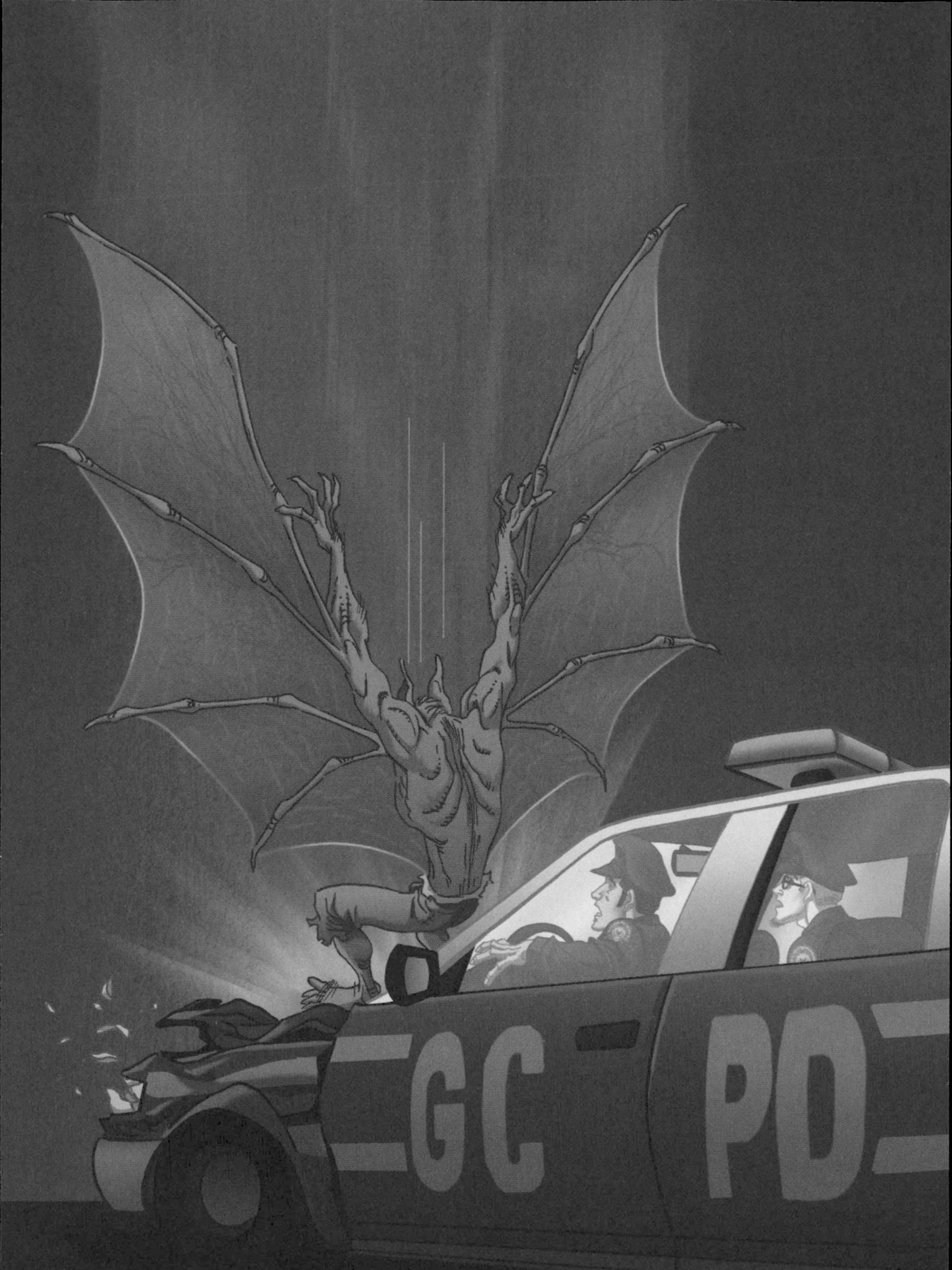
GC
PD

It was a moonless night.

Two Gotham City police officers

shouted in shock as a giant bat

landed on their patrol car.

The police officers ran for safety.

One radioed Commissioner Gordon.

"Batman just smashed our car!"

he yelled into his walkie-talkie.

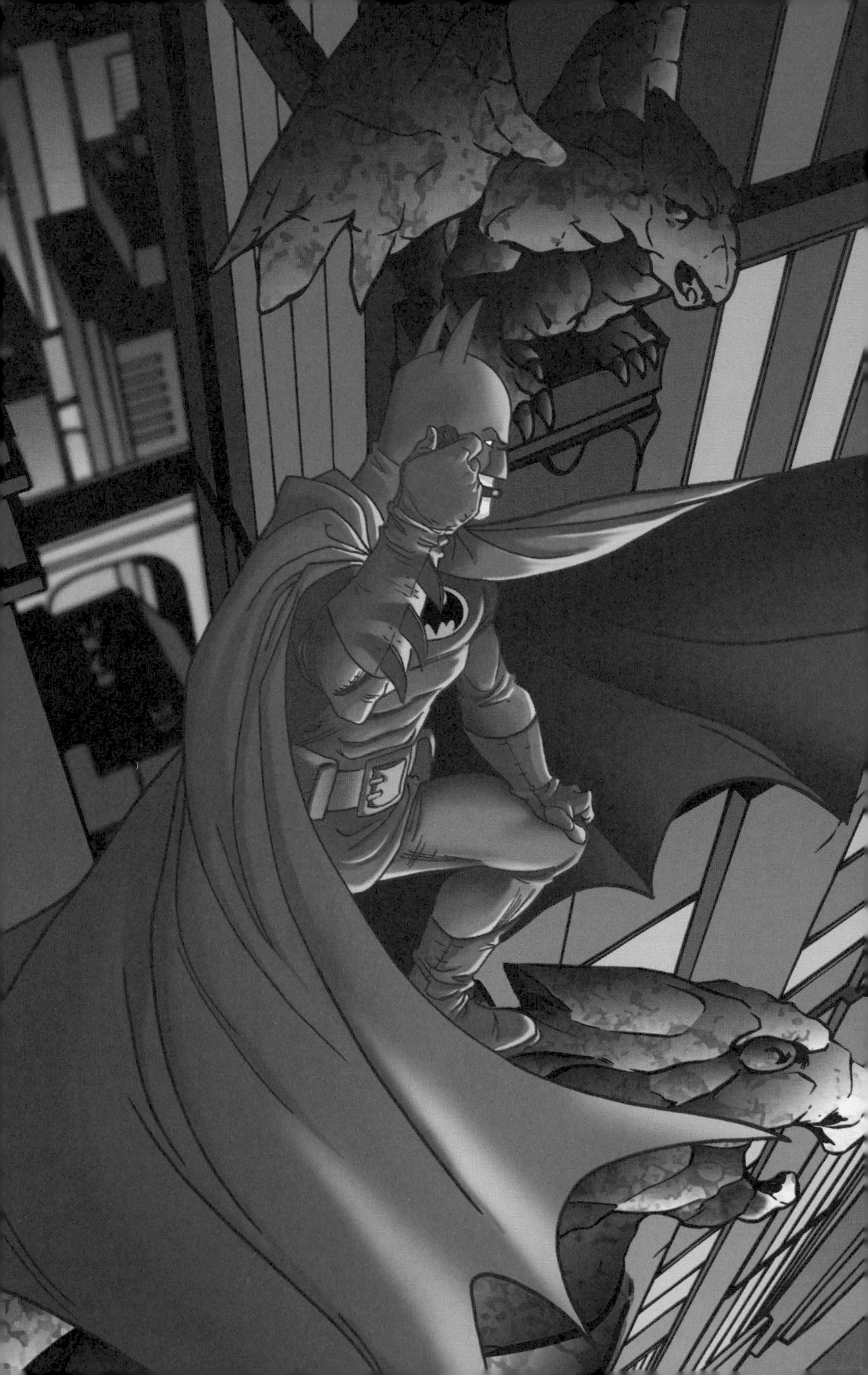

"It wasn't me," said Batman
to Commissioner Gordon.
"I see the creature now."
The strange batlike monster
tore down streetlights
throughout downtown Gotham.

Batman shot his grappling hook.

He caught the creature by the leg.

The giant bat soared into the sky,

dragging Batman with it.

Then the creature bit

through the grappling hook cable.

Batman tumbled onto a roof garden.

The creature escaped into the night.

Bruce Wayne tested the saliva

the creature left on the cable.

It was part human and part bat!

Only one scientist in Gotham

did research on animal hybrids—

Dr. Kirk Langstrom.

Alfred brought Bruce the newspaper.

The headline was BATMAN IS NOW MAN-BAT!

"I have to clear Batman's name,"

growled Bruce.

Dr. Langstrom always worked late,
so Batman visited him at night.
The Batmobile's headlights showed
Man-Bat destroying the lab!

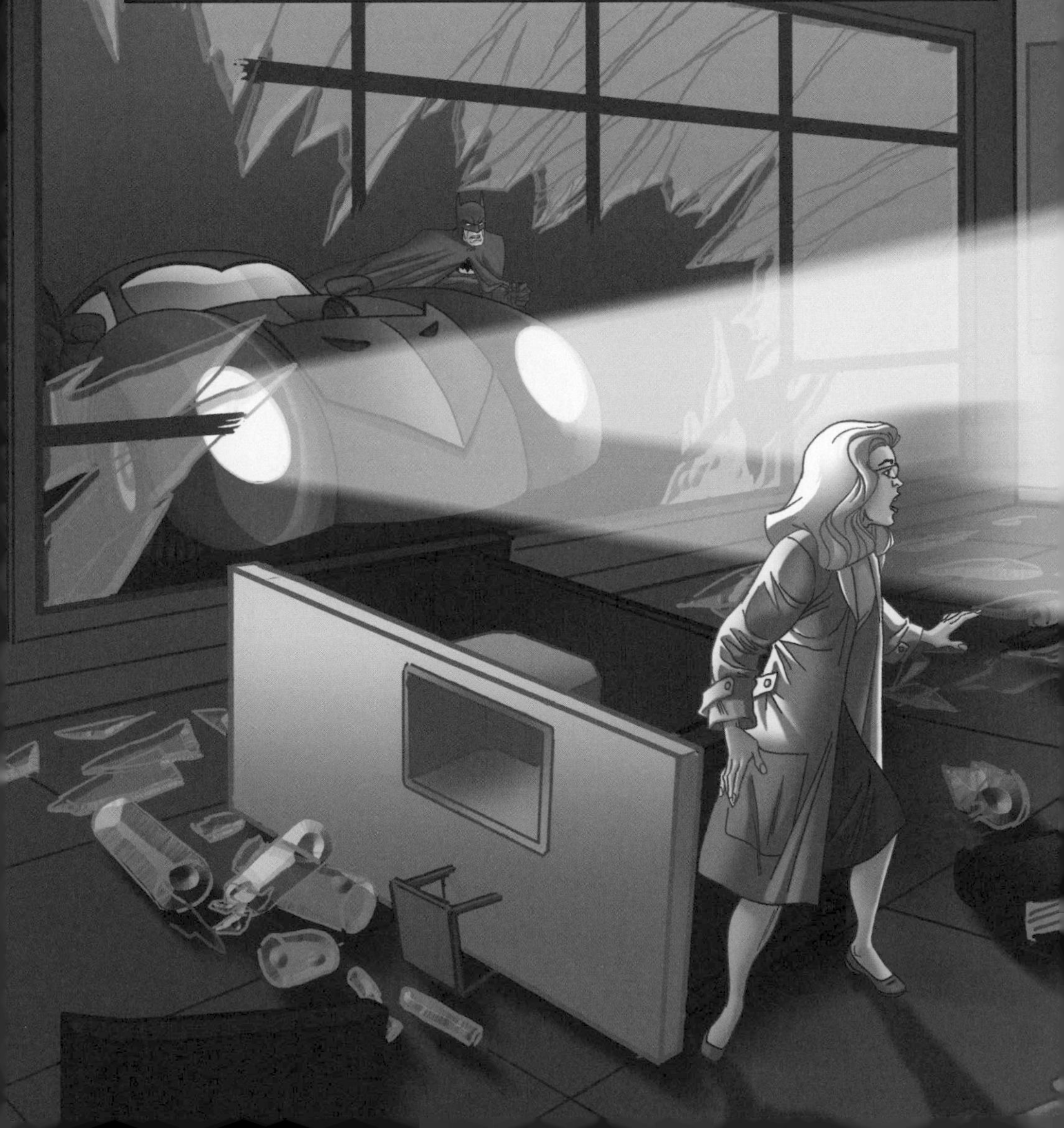

Batman raced to the rescue, leaping through the broken window to save a frightened scientist.

Man-Bat shielded his eyes
from the Batmobile's headlights.
Screaming, he burst out of the lab
through the skylight in the ceiling.

Batman spread his cape
to protect the scientist
from the falling glass.

Batman helped the scientist stand.

"Thank you for saving me," she said.

"I'm Dr. Francine Langstrom,

Kirk's wife and research partner.

That creature . . . is Kirk.

We created a DNA serum

that cured Kirk's deafness,

but it also transformed him

into that angry beast."

"Can you make an antidote?"

asked Batman. "We must save Kirk

and protect Gotham City."

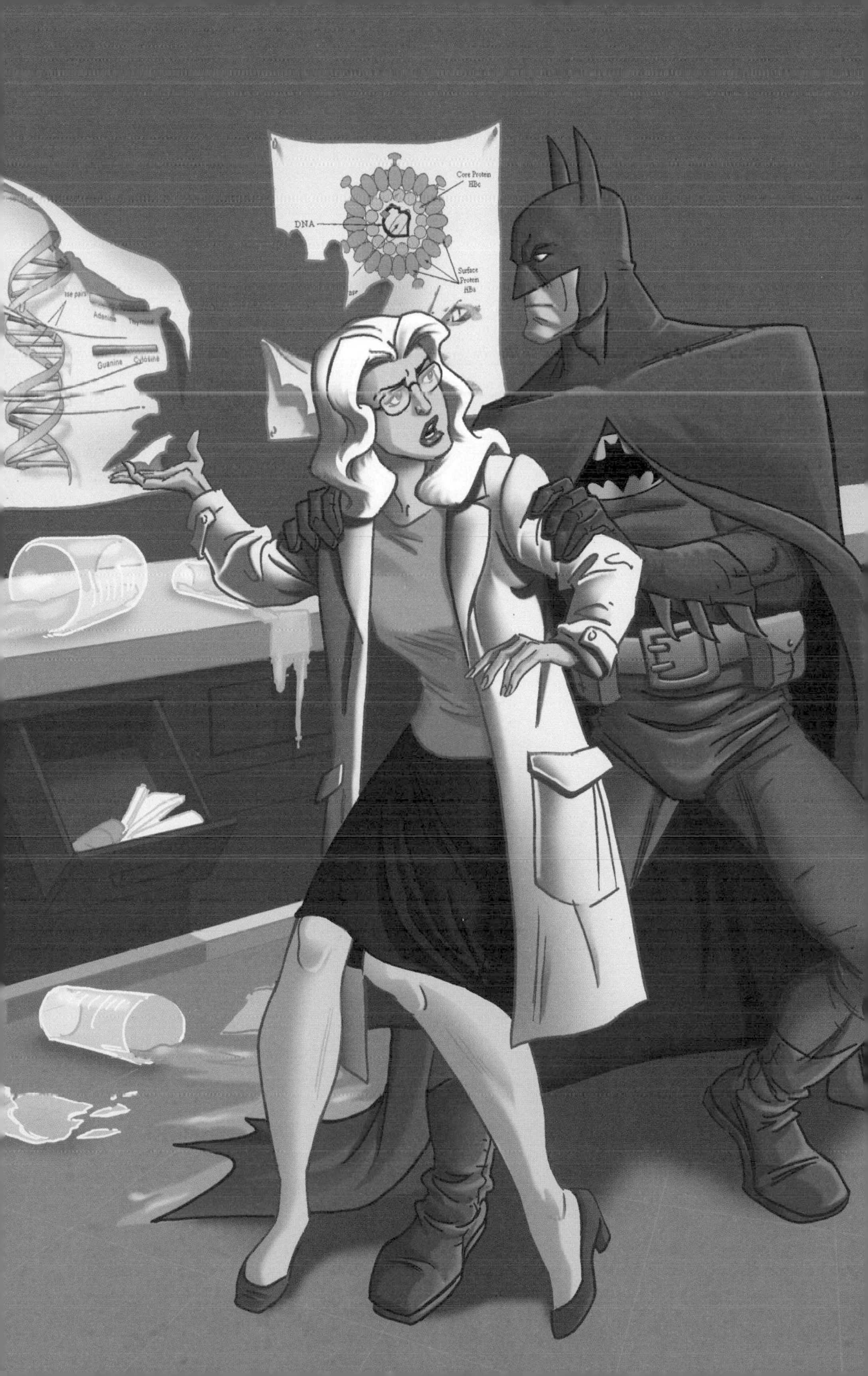
Core Protein
HBc
DNA
Surface
Protein
HBs
Adenine
Thymine
Guanine
Cytosine

Francine worked all day without stopping.

As the sun set again,

she finally came up with an antidote.

She handed it to Batman and said,

"Be careful.

He's still a human being."

Batman spotted the Bat-Signal and knew

the Commissioner needed his help.

"How can we stop this Man-Bat?"

asked Gordon.

Batman pulled out a tiny sonar device.

"Leave that to me," Batman said.

"Kill the Bat-Signal," said Batman.

Bats started to arrive,

called by the sonar device.

"Wait for my command."

Then Man-Bat appeared in the sky.

Man-Bat landed on the roof.

He screeched loudly.

His shriek was painful to Batman's
and Commissioner Gordon's ears.

Hearing the noise,

police officers ran to the roof.

They didn't know Batman was there.

They tried to stop Man-Bat on their own.

Man-Bat easily knocked the police officers

back with his powerful wings.

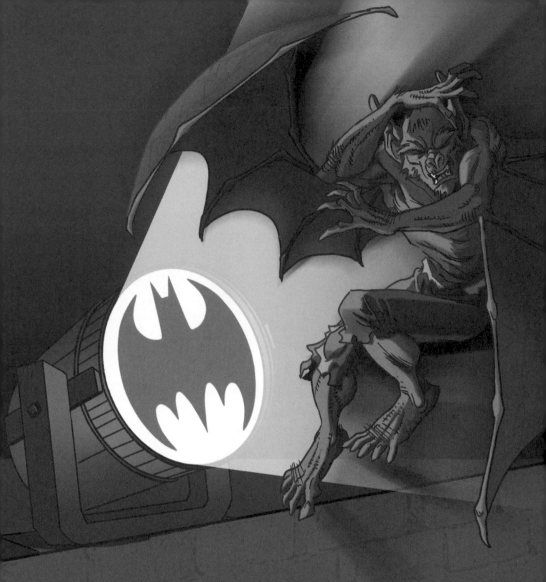

"My turn," Batman growled. "NOW!"
Commissioner Gordon flashed
the Bat-Signal directly into
Man-Bat's eyes.

Man-Bat screamed in pain
from the bright light in his eyes.
Batman wrestled him to the rooftop,
and gave him the antidote.

The antidote took effect.

Man-Bat stopped struggling.

He looked shocked.

Batman and the police watched

the amazing transformation.

Man-Bat turned back into

Dr. Kirk Langstrom.

Outside the police station,
Francine Langstrom helped
her husband into an ambulance.
The police were taking him
to the hospital for treatment.
"Congratulations, Batman,"
said Commissioner Gordon.
"You've stopped Man-Bat
and cleared your own name."
Batman shook Gordon's hand.

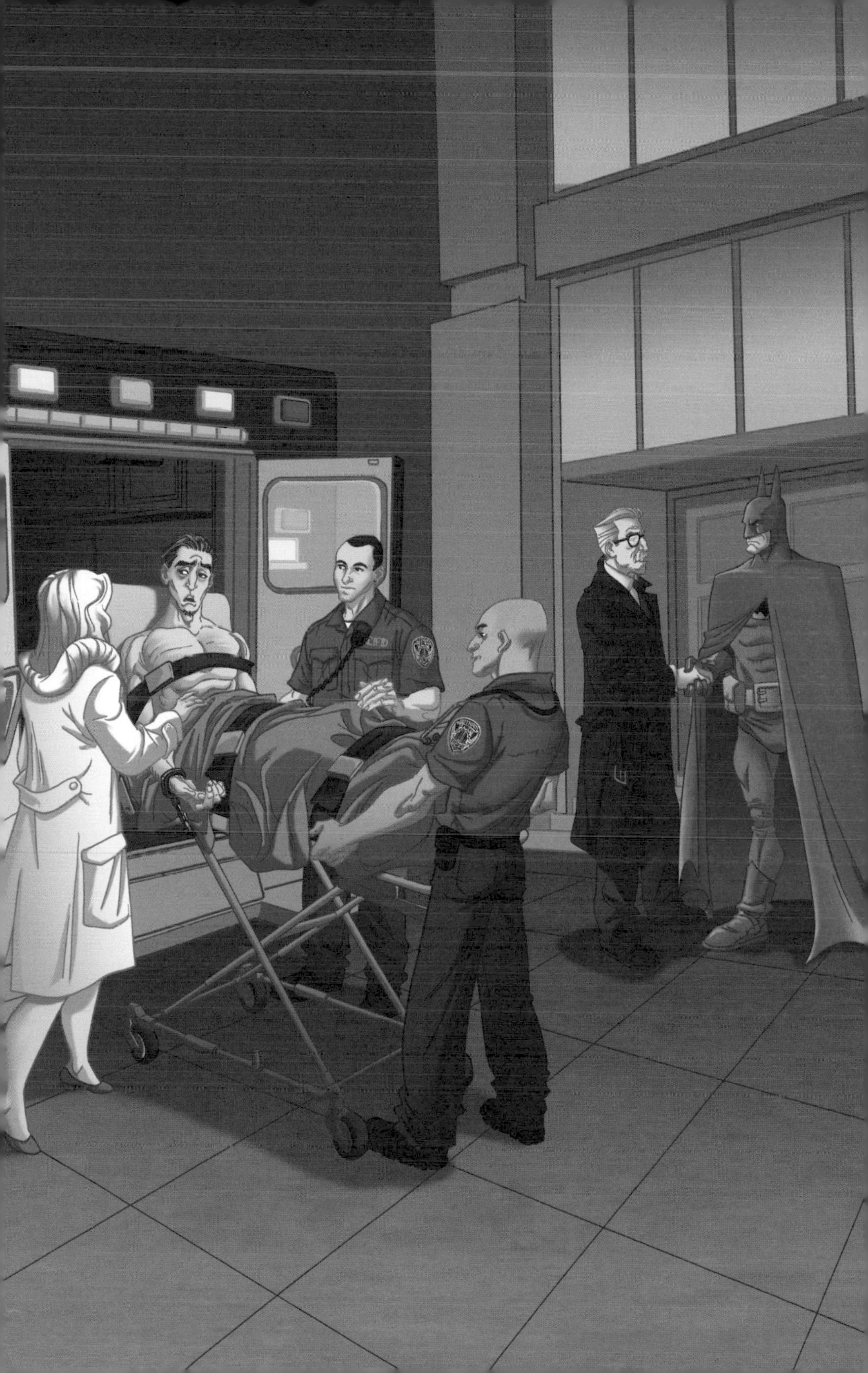

Batman swung home
over the city's rooftops.
"Good-bye, Man-Bat," said Batman.
"Gotham City already has enough
creatures of the night!"